DATE DUE

Here We Go Round the Mulberry Bush

WILL HILLENBRAND

Gulliver Books

Harcourt, Inc.

Orlando Austin New York San Diego Toronto London

Dedicated to Stergios and Ian,
friends in kindergarten—
friends forever

In special memory of my best friend, Tom

Library of Congress Cataloging-in-Publication Data
Hillenbrand, Will.
Here we go round the mulberry bush/Will Hillenbrand.
p.   cm.
"Gulliver Books."
Summary: A traditional nursery song is expanded to tell the story of a young child's first day at school.
1. Children's songs, English—United States—Texts.
[1. First day of school—Songs and music.
2. Schools—Songs and music.   3. Songs.]   I. Title.
PZ8.3.H553He   2003
782.42164'0268—dc21   2002012396
ISBN 0-15-202032-2

First edition
H G F E D C B A

Printed in Singapore

The illustrations in this book were done in mixed media on vellum, painted on both sides.
The display lettering was created by Jane Dill.
The text type was set in Bryn Mawr Medium.
Color separations by Bright Arts Ltd., Hong Kong
Printed and bound by Tien Wah Press, Singapore
This book was printed on totally chlorine-free Enso Stora Matte paper.
Production supervision by Sandra Grebenar and Pascha Gerlinger
Designed by Linda Lockowitz

Here We Go Round the Mulberry Bush

Here we go round the mul-ber-ry bush, the mul-ber-ry bush, the mul-ber-ry bush.

Here we go round the mul-ber-ry bush, on our first da-y of sch-ool.

Here we go round the mulberry bush,
  the mulberry bush, the mulberry bush.
Here we go round the mulberry bush,
on our first day of school.

This is the way we say *hello*,
say *hello,* say *hello.*
Who are all these kids that I don't know?
I'm scared of this first day of school.

Here is where we hang our hat,
hang our hat, hang our hat.
I'm leaving mine on. I really wish that
I were home instead of at school.

This is where we build a tower,
build a tower, build a tower.
Oh, how many minutes, how many hours
until we go home from school?

Here is where we splash and pour,
splash and pour, splash and pour.
I splash on myself, then pour on the floor.
It's a messy first day of school!

This is the way we play outside,
play outside, play outside.
The others play tag, while I sit and hide.
I'm lonely this first day of school.

Here they run round the mulberry bush,
the mulberry bush, the mulberry bush.
Here they run round the mulberry bush . . .

The bell rings and we dash inside,
dash inside, dash inside.
My new friend and I run side by side.
It's the first time I've smiled at school!

Now it's time to eat our snack,
eat our snack, eat our snack.
Our teacher made cookies. I ate a whole stack!
Things aren't so bad here at school.

This is where we dress and pretend,
dress and pretend, dress and pretend.
We're all little monsters! I've found more new friends.
There are kids just like me at this school.

Then our teacher reads a book,
reads a book, reads a book.
How funny and strange all those squiggly lines look!
Maybe I'll learn to read at my school.

Now it's time for show-and-tell,
show-and-tell, show-and-tell.
Did I really hear the final bell
to end the first day of school?

This is how we clean our room,
clean our room, clean our room,
at the end of the day—it came so soon?
I can't wait to come back to school!

Now it's time to say *good-bye*,
say *good-bye*, say *good-bye*.
My first day has made me one happy guy.
I'll see you tomorrow at school!

Here we go round the mulberry bush,
the mulberry bush, the mulberry bush.
Here we go round the mulberry bush,
on our way home from school.